We Can Fix It

Brrrrrrrr!!!

Written by Robbie Byerly
Illustrated by John Bianchi

2

3

4

7

8

9

Use the words you know...

and
band
sand
land
hand

dad
pad
mad
sad
glad
bad

too
tools
pool
soon
shoot
scoot

14

...to read new words!

skunk
funk
dunk
junk

ring
sing
bring
thing

cash
mash
flash
trash

Tricky Words

again

help

just

thing

us